Save the
Pet Shop!

No part of this publication may be reproduced, stored in a retrieval system, or transmitted in any form or by any means, electronic, mechanical, photocopying, recording, or otherwise, without written permission of the publisher.
For information regarding permission, write to Scholastic Inc.,
Attention: Permissions Department, 557 Broadway, New York, NY 10012.

ISBN 978-0-545-60775-9

HASBRO and its logo, BLYTHE, LITTLEST PET SHOP, and all related characters are trademarks of Hasbro and are used with permission.

Published by Scholastic Inc. SCHOLASTIC and associated logos are trademarks and/or registered trademarks of Scholastic Inc.

12 11 10 9 8 7 6 5 4 3 2 1   14 15 16 17 18 19/0

Designed by Leslie Mechanic
Printed in the U.S.A.   40
First printing, February 2014

Contents

Welcome Home!...................................1

Surprise!.......................................7

Is This a Dream?..............................12

Save the Pet Shop............................16

Blythe Style...................................26

The Show Must Go On....................31

Runway-Ready...............................35

Showstoppers 41

Chapter 1
Welcome Home!

"Here we are!" Roger Baxter announced to his daughter. "Home, sweet home!"

Blythe sat in the backseat of her dad's car. She peeked out from behind her sketchbook as he drove up the unfamiliar block.

Roger was always full of surprises. His latest? A move to Downtown City.

"You know I hate surprises, Dad," Blythe said.

"Maybe you can think of this as a great adventure!" her dad said.

Doubtful, Blythe thought. Flying planes like her pilot dad did was an adventure. Starting a new school? That was a nightmare!

As her dad parked the car, Blythe saw the tall building that would soon be their home. At street-level was a store. Its sign read LITTLEST PET SHOP!

"We're moving to a pet shop?" Blythe asked as she got out of the car.

Blythe was about to climb the front steps, when her path was blocked. Standing in front of her were identical twins. They had identical scowls on their faces!

"You startled me!" Blythe gasped. The twins shrugged. One pointed to the words on Blythe's sketchbook.

"Blythe Style?" she said. "Is that your name?"

Blythe tried not to giggle. "Blythe Style" was the name she had given her fashion designs. Her sketchbook was filled with them.

"It's Blythe Baxter," she said.

The twins introduced themselves as Whittany and Brittany Biskit.

Brittany looked Blythe up and down and asked, "Are *those* your clothes?"

"You need new ones," Whittany said. "If you want to go shopping with us, we'll let you."

Blythe gulped. These twins were snooty times two!

"No, thanks," Blythe said. "I have a lot of unpacking to do."

The twins narrowed their eyes.

"We've *never* been told no!" Brittany exclaimed.

Blythe was about to squeeze by when she heard the babble of baby talk. She glanced back and froze. Her dad was tapping on the window of the pet shop!

"*Oooh,* you are the cutest things," Roger cooed.

Hopping behind the glass were a hedgehog, skunk, monkey, gecko, panda, mongoose, and lapdog. They all seemed happy to see Roger.

Blythe was *definitely not* happy. Her dad was being a total embarrassment! She raced to stop him, but it was too late.

"Tell your father not to get used to those pets," Brittany sneered.

"Yeah," Whittany said. "Littlest Pet Shop won't be around much longer!"

Chapter 2
Surprise!

Blythe tried to forget about the mean girls as she unpacked. One of the first things out of the box was her guitar. Strumming it, Blythe began to sing:

"This is a new adventure and I really love it here. I love my new room—but it sure does need some air."

Blythe used her guitar to help press open the window. But there was no gentle breeze. Instead, a huge blast of air knocked Blythe back on her bed!

This was no window! It was a "dumbwaiter," a kind of mini elevator used to cart things up and down.

"I've heard about old buildings having these!" Blythe said.

Just then, Blythe heard music drifting up the shaft. Where was it coming from? There was only one way to find out . . . .

Blythe reached in and grabbed the rope. She pulled up the dumbwaiter car and hopped aboard.

"Now, *this* is an adventure!" Blythe declared.

She held on tight as she lowered the car. The shaft was dark. It was also loaded with dust that tickled Blythe's nose.

"*Ahh-chooo!*" Blythe sneezed.

She dropped the rope to cover her mouth and nose. That's when the dumbwaiter dropped, too.

"*Whooooaaaa!*" Blythe shouted as the dumbwaiter raced down the shaft!

Waiting for a crash, Blythe squeezed

her eyes shut. Her teeth rattled inside her head as the car finally bumped to a stop. Then, voices . . . .

"Who is she?"

"I hope she's not hurt."

A tiny finger poked Blythe's shoulder. Her eyes popped open and she gasped. The voices were coming from *animals!*

"You're a porcupine!" Blythe shouted as she pointed to the spiky creature in the bunch.

"Hedgehog, actually," he said.

Blythe stared at the animals as they stared back at her. Beside the hedgehog there was a skunk, monkey, panda, gecko, lapdog, and mongoose. They

looked like normal animals, but Blythe knew something weird was going on. Something crazy-weird!

"Animals are speaking!" Blythe cried. "And I can understand them?!"

Chapter 3
Is This a Dream?

Blythe wasn't the only one who was surprised.

"You understand what we're saying?" the skunk asked.

Blythe nodded yes. The pets all smiled. Finally, a human who could understand them!

"Do you have a name?" the gecko asked.

"*Uh* . . . B-B-Blythe," Blythe stammered.

"Hi, Blythe!" the animals declared.

A glam Spaniel padded forward and introduced herself and the others.

"I'm Zoe, and this is Pepper Clark the skunk, Vinnie Terrio the gecko, Minka Mark the monkey, Sunil Nevla the mongoose, Russell Ferguson the hedgehog, and Penny Ling the panda. We're all Day Campers at Littlest Pet Shop."

Was this a dream? Or did the dumbwaiter fall really rattle her?

"I've got to get out of here!" Blythe cried.

As Blythe ran out of the shop, a new customer walked in.

She was there to talk to the shop's owner, Mrs. Twombly. But this woman didn't want to buy kibble. She wanted to buy Littlest Pet Shop—and turn it into a sweet shop!

The pets couldn't believe their ears!

"Where will our owners take us to Day Camp?" Minka gasped.

If only someone could help them. Someone who understood them!

Russell's eyes lit up as that someone came to mind. He knew exactly whom they needed.

They needed Blythe!

Chapter 4
Save the Pet Shop

The next morning the pets used the dumbwaiter to sneak into Blythe's room. "Wake up, Blythe," Russell whispered.

Blythe's eyes fluttered open. When she saw the animals she screamed.

"It wasn't a dream!" Blythe cried. "I really can talk to animals! How is that possible?"

"We have more important things to talk about," Russell said. "We need your help."

Blythe listened to the pets' problem. She felt badly that they might lose their Day Camp. But what could she do?

Meanwhile, the pets were helping themselves to Blythe's clothes. Zoe found Blythe's sketchbook. She tore out her favorite design and held it under her chin.

"This has 'Zoe' written all over it in big, sparkly letters!" Zoe said happily.

"It does look good," Blythe said.

But there was no time to talk about saving Littlest Pet Shop or fashion. It was Blythe's first day of school.

Blythe hustled the pets back into the dumbwaiter.

"If you don't help us we'll all have to go to Largest Ever Pet Shop!" Russell begged.

Blythe got upset as Russell explained that all the pets would be sent to a huge, cold pet store. It had no toys, no play areas, and no heart!

"Okay, I'll help." Blythe sighed. "I have no idea how, but I'll think of something."

"We only have until tomorrow!" the pets cried.

Blythe had to think fast!

The pets zoomed down the shaft. As soon as they touched down they began to brainstorm. How could they help

Blythe save Littlest
Pet Shop?

"Hold a show
with lots of great
singers!" Zoe belted
out. "Like *meeeee!*"

"A comedy show
will pack them in,"
Pepper said. "I'll be
the headliner!"

"Maybe Blythe
can make Mrs.
Twombly's problems
disappear!" Sunil
suggested while wearing a magician's
top hat.

"What if we have a dance-a-thon?!" Vinnie said, before tripping over his own feet.

Russell groaned as everyone spoke at once. At this rate they would get nowhere.

At school Blythe was getting nowhere with her new locker. Luckily, three classmates named Jasper, Sue, and Youngmee came to the rescue. Once they opened her locker, Blythe introduced herself.

She said that she had just moved into the same building as Littlest Pet Shop.

She explained how the shop would be closing and that the pets would be moved to a terrible place.

Sue told Blythe that Largest Ever Pet Shop was owned by Whittany and Brittany Biskit's family. No wonder the store was bad news!

Later in the lunchroom Blythe sat

with her new friends. Blythe drew happily in her sketchbook—until it was snatched out of her hands!

"Blythe Style?" Whittany sneered as she flipped through it. "More like Blech Style."

"If you want to sit at our table," Brittany said snootily, "we'll allow it."

Allow it? Blythe gritted her teeth. As if she would even want to sit with them!

"I'm sitting with my new friends," Blythe said. "So, no thanks."

What?? Steam seemed to flow out of the twins' ears. Did Blythe just say no to them *again?*

"You just got on our bad side," Whittany warned.

Then the two mean girls scattered Blythe's sketches all over the floor.

As the Biskits stormed off, Blythe picked up a torn page. It was Zoe's favorite design. Blythe studied it, then smiled to herself.

"Those Biskits may be mean,"

Blythe said. "But they just gave me a great idea. I know how to save Littlest Pet Shop!"

Chapter 5
Blythe Style

After school, Blythe raced to Littlest Pet Shop. She had to talk to the shop owner, Mrs. Twombly.

"Blythe looks excited," Minka whispered.

With the help of Zoe's sensitive hearing, the pets listened to Blythe's conversation.

"I know how to save Littlest Pet Shop!" Blythe said. She held up her sketchbook. "I never thought of designing pet clothes until today. But

I was thinking if we could put on a fashion show—"

"A fashion show!" Zoe whispered to the pets. This was right up her alley, and she wasn't even a cat!

Blythe went on with her plan. They would use the Day Camp pets as models. People would come for the show and fall in love with the shop. There would be tons of new customers.

"Let's do it!" said Mrs. Twombly.

Blythe's heart did a triple flip. Her dream of becoming a fashion designer was coming true.

But there was no time for cartwheels. Blythe had to make her designs runway-ready lickety-split.

With the help of the pets, Blythe's bedroom became a fashion workroom. Blythe sketched. The pets cut and stitched the fabrics.

When the fashions were ready, it was time to spread the word about the show. Blythe rode through town with a basketful of fliers. The pets helped, hanging them all over Downtown City.

Before long, everyone knew about the Blythe Style Fashion Show at Littlest Pet Shop.

Everyone including Whittany and Brittany Biskit.

"This is a good idea," Brittany sneered.

"Yeah," Whittany said as she ripped down the flier. "And we've got to do something to *ruin* it!"

Chapter 6
The Show Must Go On

Finally, it was showtime! Outside Littlest Pet Shop, there was a runway and a stage. People and their pets filled every seat.

"Blythe, that's some crowd out there," Mrs. Twombly said.

Blythe was happy to see a full house. She was also happy to see her new besties, Jasper, Sue, and Youngmee!

"Blythe, you're a genius," Jasper said. "But how are you going to come up with all that money?"

"What money?" Blythe asked.

Jasper held up one of Blythe's fliers. Blythe gasped at the words *Come Get Free Money!*

"Who could have added those words to our fliers?" Blythe wondered. "It's so mean!"

Mean? Mean meant two things: Whittany and Brittany Biskit!

But the money rumor was just Step One of the twins' mean plan. Step Two was in the works.

"Remind me why we're dressed like icky cats?" Brittany whispered.

"We're undercover," Whittany told her. "So we need to blend in with the other pets in the fashion show."

The twins climbed the ladder to the catwalk above the stage. Roped around their waists were buckets of kitty litter and chocolate sauce. They were going to dump the yucky stuff on Blythe!

Meanwhile, the crowd was getting restless. They wanted their free money.

"I have some good news and some bad news," Mrs. Twombly announced. "The bad news is . . . there is no free money."

"Awwww!" The crowd groaned.

"The good news is," Mrs. Twombly said, "the first ever Littlest Pet Shop fashion show is about to begin!"

Chapter 7
Runway-Ready

"You're all going to be great," Blythe told the pets backstage. "Remember, be yourselves!"

"Places, everybody," Russell announced. He was the stage manager. "This is it!"

The pets were excited! They were wearing fashionable outfits that celebrated each of their talents.

Russell cued the music. The crowd *ooh*ed and *ahh*ed as the pets pranced down the runway.

"Those pet fashions are really cutting-edge!" a woman declared.

Vinnie danced across the stage in a white suit and sparkly glove.

Sunil's splashy rain gear got super-sunny smiles.

Minka painted the town in a cool artist's smock and beret.

Then came Penny in a cute kimono-inspired dress.

Finally, Pepper got the last laugh in a clown suit and pink wig.

Sweet! Russell thought as he watched his friends. But then he noticed something fishy going on above the stage. He looked up and saw a bucket being yanked up the side of the scaffold by a rope!

Meanwhile, out on the runway it was time for the big finish. Everyone went wild when they saw Zoe.

She was sparkling from head to paw. Blythe's fashions were a hit!

"You need to go out and take a bow, Blythe!" Mrs. Twombly urged.

"I think I will!" Blythe smiled. At the same time Russell scurried up the scaffold. He spotted two catty-looking figures holding buckets.

"Whittany, I'm getting tired," Brittany whined. "Can we, like, dump out this stuff now?"

"In a second, Brittany," Whittany snapped. "It's got to be at just the right moment."

Right moment? Russell glanced down to see Blythe taking the stage.

"This will teach Blythe never to say no to us!" Whittany snickered.

Russell gasped as the girls began tipping their buckets over the rail.

They were about to dump something on Blythe. And he had a feeling it wasn't confetti!

Chapter 8
Showstoppers

Russell came to the rescue. He tucked himself into a ball and rolled across the catwalk. The twins shrieked as Russell popped out of his ball and barked.

"A porcupine!" Brittany yelled.

Whittany screamed, too. The twins lost their balance, toppling backward over the rail!

"I'm a hedgehog!" Russell shouted after them.

Ropes still around their waists, the twins plummeted toward the ground.

"Ahhhhhhh!" they shouted.

Their drop came to a sudden stop. Whittany and Brittany kept screaming as they dangled in midair. When they glanced down, they sighed with relief. They were only inches off the ground! The twins stepped down. As they untied the ropes, the buckets on the catwalk began to topple. Until—

SPLAT!

Whittany and Brittany were covered with globs of chocolate sauce and kitty litter—all meant for Blythe!

The twins were furious. They charged off the runway and down the street, screaming all the way!

Blythe and the pets took their bows at last. The fashion show had been saved. And so had Littlest Pet Shop!

Later, Mrs. Twombly beamed as she rang up the last sale of the day.

"All these sales!" Mrs. Twombly said. "Blythe, the only way I'll be able to keep up is if you work for me."

"Really?" Blythe asked. "I'd love to."

The pets were thrilled, too. They would get to see— and talk to — Blythe every day.

The next day a brand-new sign went up in the store window: Blythe Style Sold Exclusively At Littlest Pet Shop!

Blythe was tickled pink. Her dream of becoming a fashion designer had come true. Her dad was right— Downtown City had turned out to be full of adventure. All thanks to a store called Littlest Pet Shop . . . and some totally talented, *awesome* new friends!